The Pirate Meets the Queen

An illuminated tale by

Matt Faulkner

PHILOMEL BOOKS • NEW YORK

there are as many ways to spell O'Malley as there are O'Malleys. Even the O'Malley clan spelled their names different ways. One tombstone spelling in County Mayo is U'Mallie; in this book the author selects the popular spelling of O'Mally for the tombstone, but selects the more commonly used and agreed upon spelling of O'Malley to tell his story.

Patricia Lee Gauch, Editor

PHILOMEL BOOKS
A division of Penguin Young Readers Group   Published by The Penguin Group
Penguin Group (USA) Inc., 375 Hudson Street, New York, NY 10014, U.S.A.
Penguin Group (Canada), 10 Alcorn Avenue, Toronto, Ontario, Canada M4V 3B2 (a division of Pearson Penguin Canada Inc.)
Penguin Books Ltd, 80 Strand, London WC2R 0RL, England.
Penguin Ireland, 25 St. Stephen's Green, Dublin 2, Ireland (a division of Penguin Books Ltd.)
Penguing Group (Australia), 250 Camberwell Road, Camberwell, Victoria 3124, Australia (a division of Pearson Australia Group Pty Ltd)
Penguin Books India Pvt Ltd, 11 Community Centre, Panchsheel Park, New Delhi - 110 017, India.
Penguin Group (NZ), Cnr Airborne and Rosedale Roads, Albany, Auckland 1310, New Zealand (a division of Pearson New Zealand Ltd.)
Penguin Books (South Africa) (Pty) Ltd, 24 Sturdee Avenue, Rosebank, Johannesburg 2196, South Africa.
Penguin Books Ltd, Registered Offices: 80 Strand, London WC2R 0RL, England.

Manufactured in China by South China Printing Co. Ltd.   Design by Semadar Megged.   Text set in 15.5-point Galena.
The art was rendered in gouache on Arches 140-lb cold press watercolor paper.
Library of Congress Cataloging-in-Publication Data
Faulkner, Matt.   The pirate meets the queen / Matt Faulkner.   p. cm.   Summary: When the son of notorious Irish pirate queen Granny O'Malley is captured by the English, Granny tries to meet with Queen Elizabeth I to negotiate for his freedom.   1. O'Malley, Grace, 1530?–1603?—Juvenile fiction. [1. O'Malley, Grace, 1530?–1603?—Fiction. 2. Pirates—Fiction. 3. Elizabeth, I, Queen of England 1533–1603—Fiction.] I. Title.
PZ7.F2765Pi 2005   [E]—dc22   2004010419   ISBN 0-399-24038-1
10 9 8 7 6 5 4 3 2 1
First Impression

To my parents, Ruth and Brud.   —M.F.

'Tis very odd, you know, the things they say about you after you've been dead awhile. I've heard the tales they tell. Some call me a pirate. Others call me a hero. Truth is, I was neither a pirate nor a hero. Just a red-haired Irish woman who did things because she wanted to or had to. No more, no less.

I was born in Kildawnet Castle on a stormy day in the spring of 1530. My ma said my wailing could wake the dead. They called me Granuaile. Granny for short. My ma's name was Meg—my da, Black Oak, chief of the O'Malleys.

The O'Malleys were a proud people. Peaceful fishermen. However, if times were lean, we'd raise a pirate's flag and hunt for English merchant ships. Once aboard, we'd take everything that wasn't nailed down. Unless, of course, we needed the nails.

From my first day on board, I was enchanted
by the sea. By the age of seven I sailed with
Black Oak on his fighting galley, the *Stallion*,
and I yearned to captain my own ship one day.

But my ma had other plans. Not long after
my fifteenth birthday, I spied her marching
down to the docks. "Granny O'Malley!" she
shouted. "'Tis time ye learned the ways of a
wife!" She dragged me off to the kitchens!

That night, I chopped off my hair, dressed myself as a boy and snuck aboard the *Stallion*. We were far out to sea before anyone caught on to my disguise!

My ma was a stubborn woman, though! Soon she married me off to "Long" Donal O'Flaherty, the son of a chief. Everyone said it was a fine match, but not for me! He was a fierce man and no husband. A year to the day after we wed, I kicked Donal out of his own castle and bolted the door. That was the end of my first marriage.

When Black Oak grew too old for the sea, he gave his ship to me. At last, captain of my own ship! Most of the crew came along, but some didn't, me being a woman. The English had become a thorn in our Irish sides, so I raised the pirate's flag and took pleasure in plundering fat English merchant ships.

But this time my mischief ruffled the feathers of none other than Red Liz, Queen of England. She declared me an outlaw and ordered her ships and soldiers to hunt me down. I was too smart for the English dogs, but not so the rest of the O'Malleys.

The English turned to attacking my kin. They burned our villages and crops. They sank our boats and scattered our sheep. Our men were put in jail and their families left to starve. I gathered what was left of the tribe and took them away to a hidden castle. I swore I'd never forgive Red Liz.

'Twas a hard time for the O'Malleys, but by
hook and by crook we survived. In those first
days, I gave up pirating—my family needed me—
and in my fortieth year I married "Iron" Richard
Bourke. We soon had a baby boy. I called him
"Toby of the Boats." I loved him dearly and
spoiled him rotten.

At seventeen, Toby became the captain of his own ship! He was a fine sailor, but reckless.

Late one night, I got terrible news. Toby had been captured while attacking an English ship. They'd locked him away in a dungeon. There was talk they might hang him!

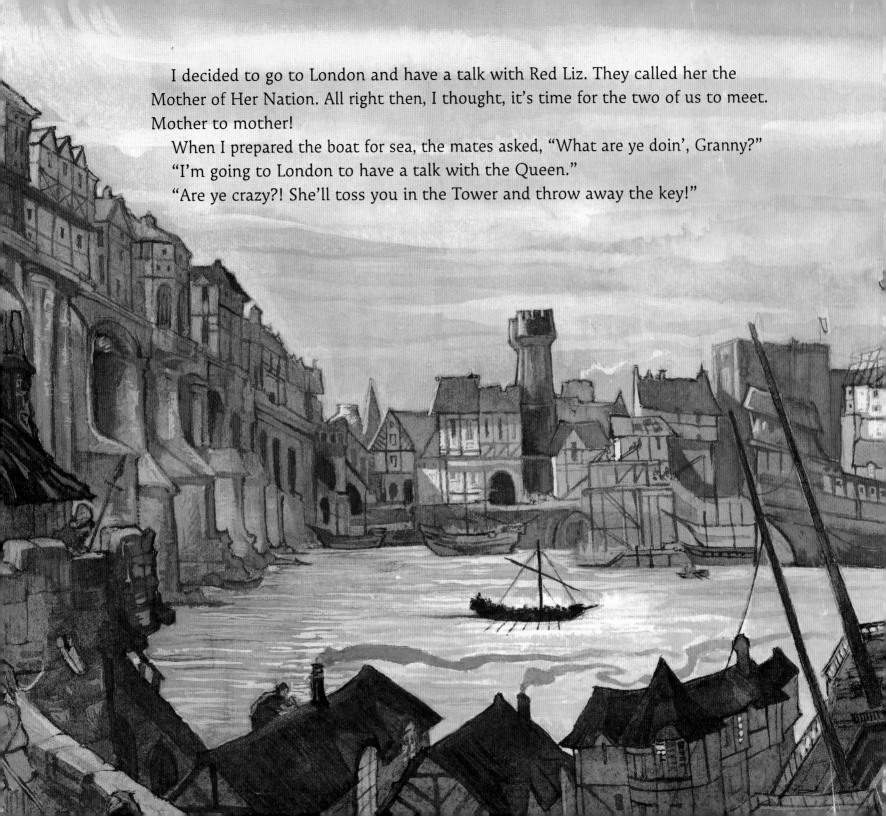

I decided to go to London and have a talk with Red Liz. They called her the Mother of Her Nation. All right then, I thought, it's time for the two of us to meet. Mother to mother!

When I prepared the boat for sea, the mates asked, "What are ye doin', Granny?"

"I'm going to London to have a talk with the Queen."

"Are ye crazy?! She'll toss you in the Tower and throw away the key!"

"'Tis the only way to set Toby free. Now, who's got the heart to come with me?!" The lads grumbled a bit, but soon they were tugging on ropes and pulling on the oars.

In a fortnight we came upon the most amazing sight of all—London!

The home of Red Liz. I found a snug place to tie the boat and hopped ashore. 'Twas like a mountain of houses. And so many people! I went from one to the next, asking for directions to the Queen. I spoke as plain as can be, but no one seemed to understand.

By the end of the day I was no closer to Red Liz than when I'd started.

I'd found a quiet corner to rest for the night when suddenly I heard a cry! Across the square I saw two young toughs robbing an old gent. I ran over, grabbed ahold of the surly pups and knocked their heads together.

"Thank you, thank you," said the old gent. "Allow me to introduce myself. I am Lord Cecil, Advisor to the Queen. How may I repay your heroic deed?"

I told Lord Cecil my story. "Tomorrow we shall visit the Queen," he said. "But tonight, you shall be my guest."

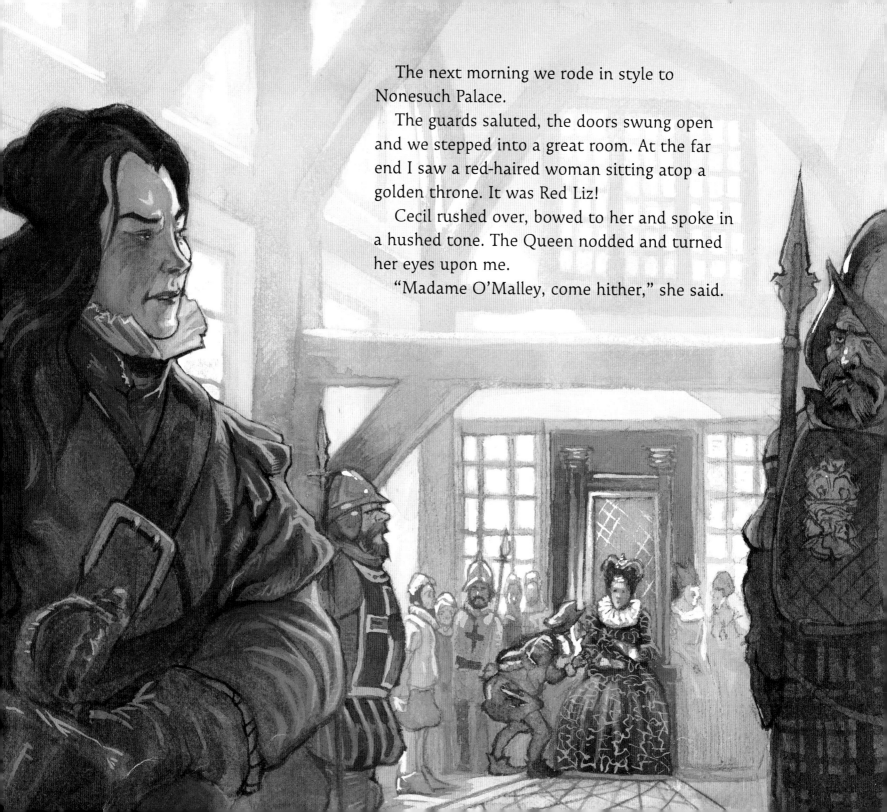

The next morning we rode in style to Nonesuch Palace.

The guards saluted, the doors swung open and we stepped into a great room. At the far end I saw a red-haired woman sitting atop a golden throne. It was Red Liz!

Cecil rushed over, bowed to her and spoke in a hushed tone. The Queen nodded and turned her eyes upon me.

"Madame O'Malley, come hither," she said.

I stepped closer.

"We applaud your bravery in saving Lord Cecil's life. He is most dear to us."

"'Twas nothing, Your Majesty."

"We think not," she replied. Then she stopped. She seemed puzzled. "O'Malley . . . ?" she murmured. "Not the Pirate O'Malley who ravaged my ships all those years ago?"

What could I do but tell the truth?

"'Tis I, Your Grace. None other."
"Indeed!" She scowled. "Well, what do you have to say for yourself?"
I couldn't think of a thing to say.
Just then, I sneezed.

I wiped my nose on my sleeve.

"No, no, no!" said the Queen, and she gave me a silken hanky.

I blew my nose and tossed the hanky into the fireplace.

"My hanky!" cried the Queen. She stared at me with icy blue eyes. "In England, one does not toss a silken hanky into the fire after a single use!"

Queen or not, no one talked to me like that!

"Is that so, Your Majesty? Well, in Ireland it'd be an insult to return a dirty nose rag to a friend!" Things weren't turning out so well. The Queen and I sounded like a couple of fish peddlers brawling in the streets. But then Liz started to laugh! Great peals of laughter were coming out of her. I started to laugh too.

After a while, the Queen put her arm in mine. "It seems that I have found a woman of consequence."

"Let's take a stroll through my garden," Liz suggested. "We have much to talk about."

So, we went for a walk—the Pirate and the Queen. Eventually, the talk came round to Toby. "Toby's a rascal," I said, "but I love him. As his mother, I'm asking you to set him free. If someone has to go to jail, let it be me."

"My dear Granny," said Liz. "'Tis a hard world filled with hard men in which we rule. I'd be a fool to put a friend such as you in a dungeon. I shall give both you and your Toby your freedom. But you must never again raise your pirate flag against my ships."

I promised. We shook on the deal. I ran all the way back to the *Stallion*.

The journey home went quickly. Upon reaching Ireland, I rushed straight to Toby's prison and was promptly arrested! The English Governor didn't believe I'd made a visit to Red Liz.

"You are a pirate," he said with a cold laugh. "And pirates tell lies."

What a sad turn of events! Locked up in the dungeon after all.

But who should I find chained to the wall beside me—my very own Toby!

Our future looked dreary indeed until the next day when the jailer flung the door open and set us free. The Queen had sent a royal courier with a letter to the English Governor the day after I'd left London!

Dear old Liz.

Ah, freedom! What a grand thing it was to be home with Toby and family and friends all around. I was tired. I promised myself that I'd stay close to my cottage and never raise the pirate flag for the rest of my days.

But I didn't keep my promise.

Things being as they were, and me being who I was, I just couldn't stay away from the sea. Back on board the *Stallion*, I did my best to keep my word to Liz and raid only those ships that didn't belong to her.

But my eyes weren't what they used to be, and I found it hard to tell one ship from another.

I pirated one or two of her lovely little merchant ships. She had so many. I am sure she didn't miss them.

AUTHOR'S NOTE

I came across the fantastic life story of Granny, or Granuaile (grahn-wale-eh), O'Malley in the summer of 2001 on a trip to Ireland. It's no secret that Ireland has more than its share of great stories. They've got tales of gods and giants and heroes, forlorn lovers and mischievous faerie folk (large and small), witches, banshees (very scary ghosts that howl through the night), talking ravens, floating churches. You name it, they've got it.

And yet, on the day before I was to head back home, I still wasn't satisfied with the stories I'd dug up. So, I did what I do whenever I'm confronted with this sort of situation: I went for a walk and got lost. I eventually found myself on a hill overlooking Dublin. Close by, I found a lovely Norman keep, which belonged to the Earl of Howth.

Knocking on the back door of the Earl's castle, I was greeted by the caretaker, who told me that I was knocking upon the very same door that the Pirate O'Malley had knocked down four hundred years earlier. I was then given a full account of that long-ago drama. Needless to say, before he had finished telling me the story, I was hooked.

After some research, I found that Granny's adventure on the Hill of Howth was just a small chapter in her glorious story. I couldn't wait to get back home and start working. I will be honest and tell you that some of what I've written is true and some of it is a little fanciful. It's the way of storytelling.

SELECTED SOURCES

Bowden, Stuart. *Ireland: A Celebration of History and Heritage*. Stamford, CT: Longmeadow Press, 1996.

Chambers, Anne. *Granuaile: The Life and Times of Grace O'Malley, c. 1530–1603*. Dublin: Wolfhound Press, 1998.

Cornish, Paul. *Henry VIII's Army*. London: Osprey, 1987.

Durham, Keith. *The Border Reivers*. London: Osprey, 1995.

Erwitt, Jennifer, and Tom Lawlor. *A Day in the Life of Ireland*. San Francisco: Collins, 1991.

Goff, Lee. *Tudor Style: Tudor Revival Houses in America from 1890 to the Present*. New York: Universe, 2002.

Grundy, Valerie, and Breandán Ó Croinin. *The Oxford Pocket Irish Dictionary*. Oxford: Oxford University Press, 2000.

Heath, Ian. *The Irish Wars, 1485–1603*. London: Osprey, 1993.

Impey, Edward, and Geoffrey Parnell. *The Tower of London: The Official Illustrated History*. London: Merrell Limited, 2000.

Jenkins, Elizabeth. *Elizabeth the Great*. New York: Coward-McCann, 1958.

Kampion, Drew. *The Book of Waves*. Santa Barbara, CA: Arpel, 1989.

Konstam, Angus. *The Armada Campaign, 1588*. London: Osprey, 2001.

——. *Elizabethan Sea Dogs, 1560–1605*. London: Osprey, 2000.

——. *The History of Pirates*. New York: Lyons Press, 1999.

——. *Renaissance War Galley, 1470–1590*. London: Osprey, 2002.

Llywelyn, Morgan. *A Pocket History of Irish Rebels*. Dublin: O'Brien Press, 2000.

Nance, R. Morton. *Classic Sailing-Ship Models in Photographs*. Mineola, NY: Dover, 2000.

O'Connor, Richard. *The Irish: Portrait of a People*. New York: G. P. Putnam's Sons, 1971.

Strong, Roy. *Gloriana: The Portraits of Queen Elizabeth I*. London: Pimlico, 1987.

Sullivan, Jonah. *Ireland*. New York: Gallery Books, 1990.

Uris, Jill, and Leon Uris. *Ireland: A Terrible Beauty*. Garden City, NY: Doubleday, 1975.

Woodward, G.W.O. *Queen Elizabeth I*. London: Pitkin, 1975.

Youngs, Susan. *The Work of Angels: Masterpieces of Celtic Metalwork, 6th–9th Centuries A.D.* Austin: University of Texas Press, 1990.